WINGED FANTASY DESIGNS
COLORING BOOK

AARON POCOCK

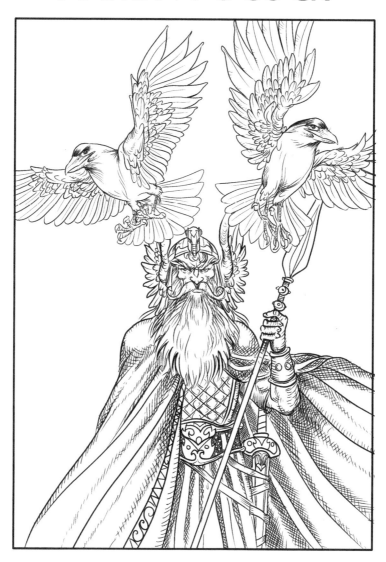

DOVER PUBLICATIONS, INC.
MINEOLA, NEW YORK

This exciting coloring book features thirty-one illustrations of winged creatures from the world of fantasy. They include dragons, elves, fairies, demons, and warriors of the sky. Intended especially for the advanced colorist, these images will help your imagination soar. In addition, the pages are perforated and are printed on one side only for easy removal and display.

Bibliographical Note
Winged Fantasy Designs Coloring Book is a new work, first published by Dover Publications, Inc., in 2016.

International Standard Book Number
ISBN-13: 978-0-486-80887-1
ISBN-10: 0-486-80887-4

Manufactured in the United States by LSC Communications
80887404   2018
www.doverpublications.com

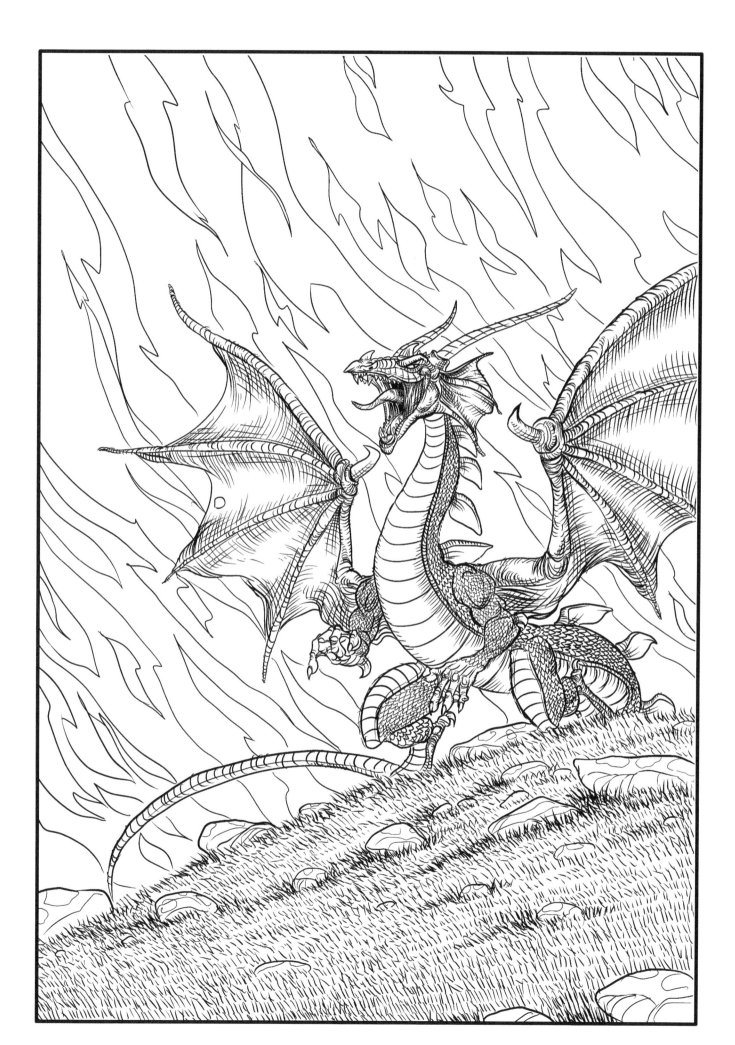

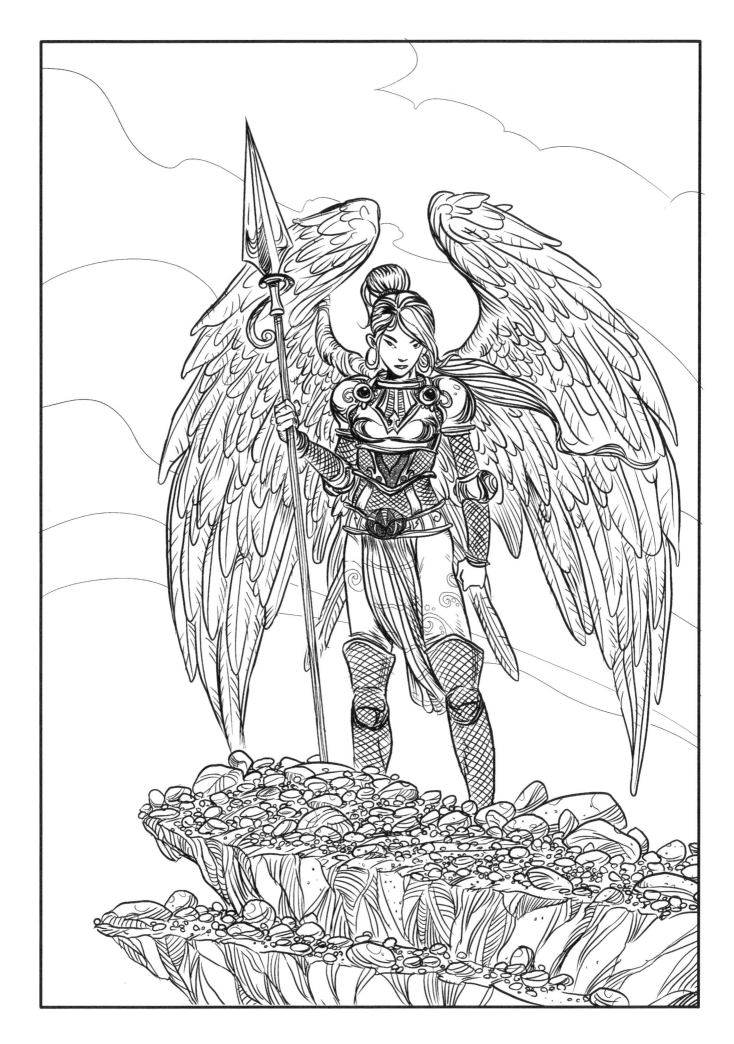

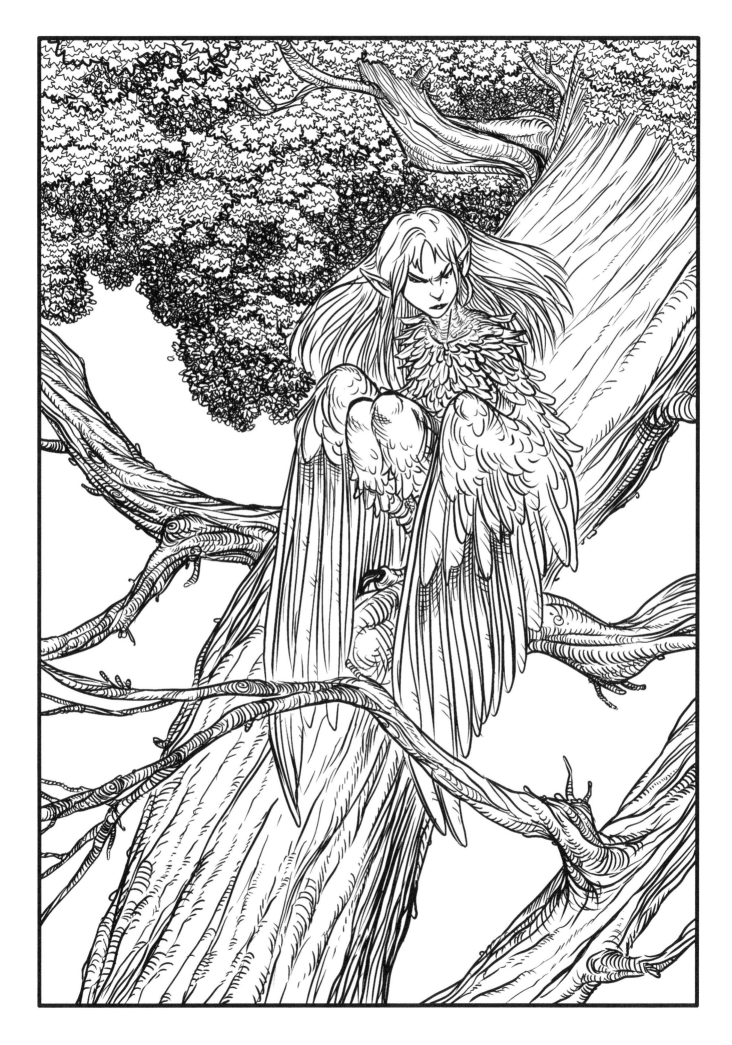

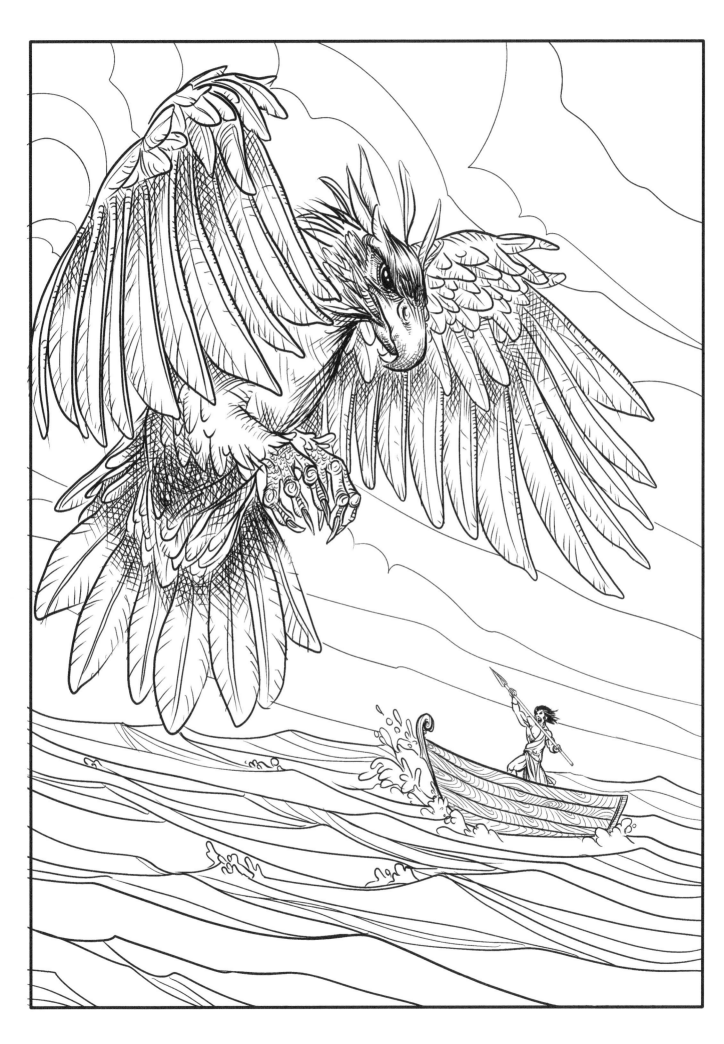

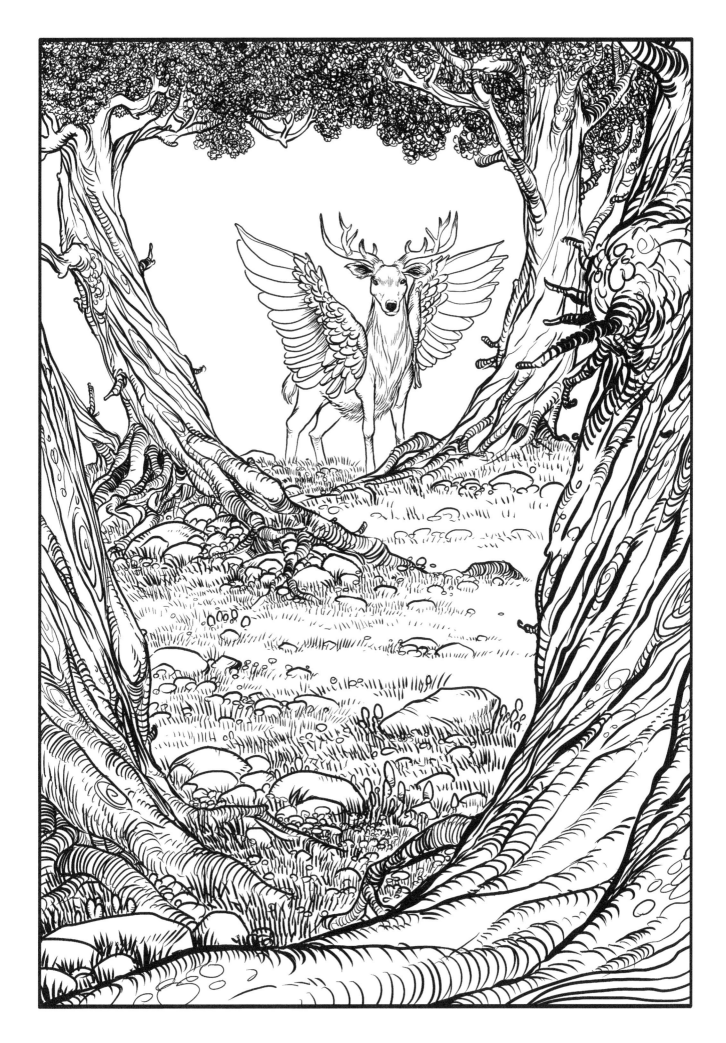

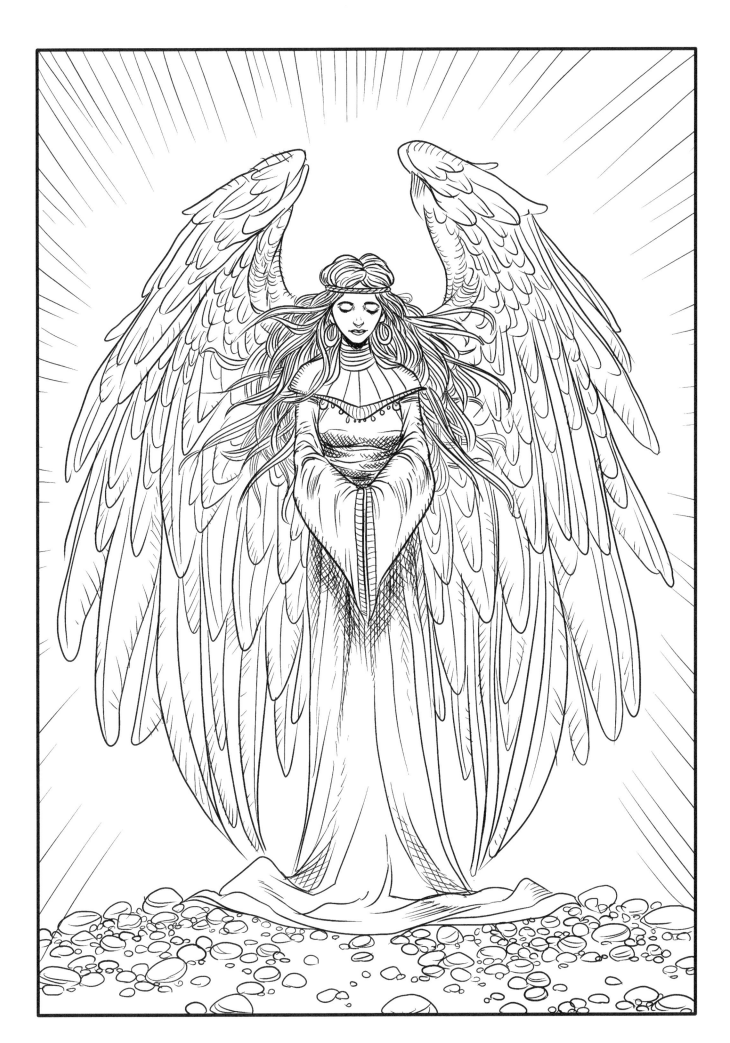

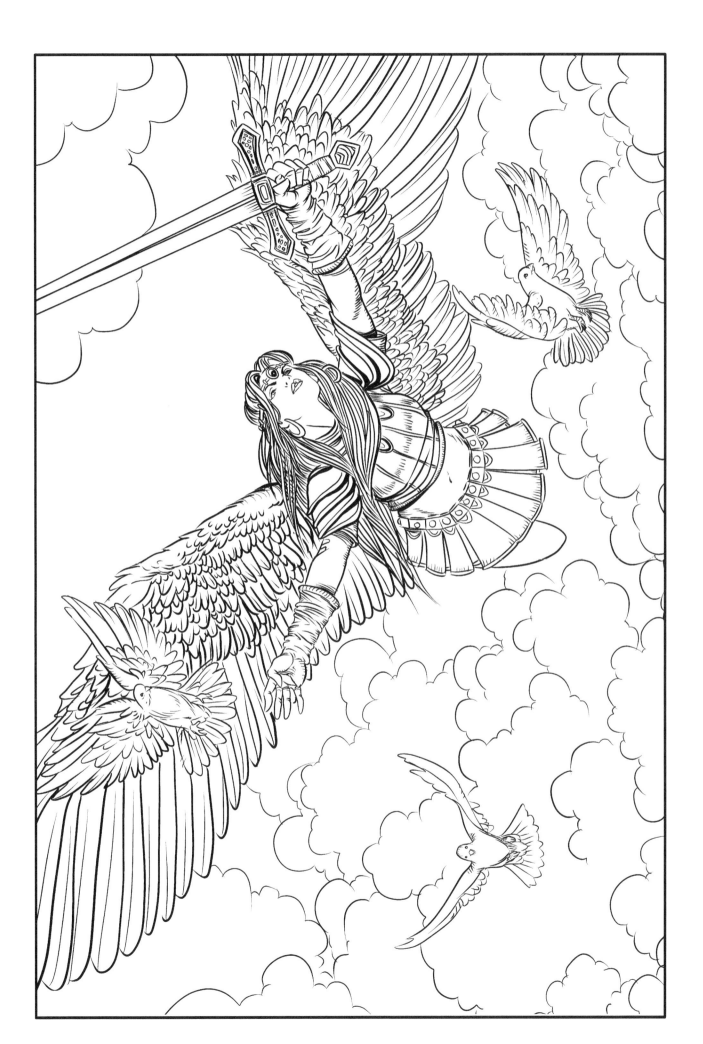

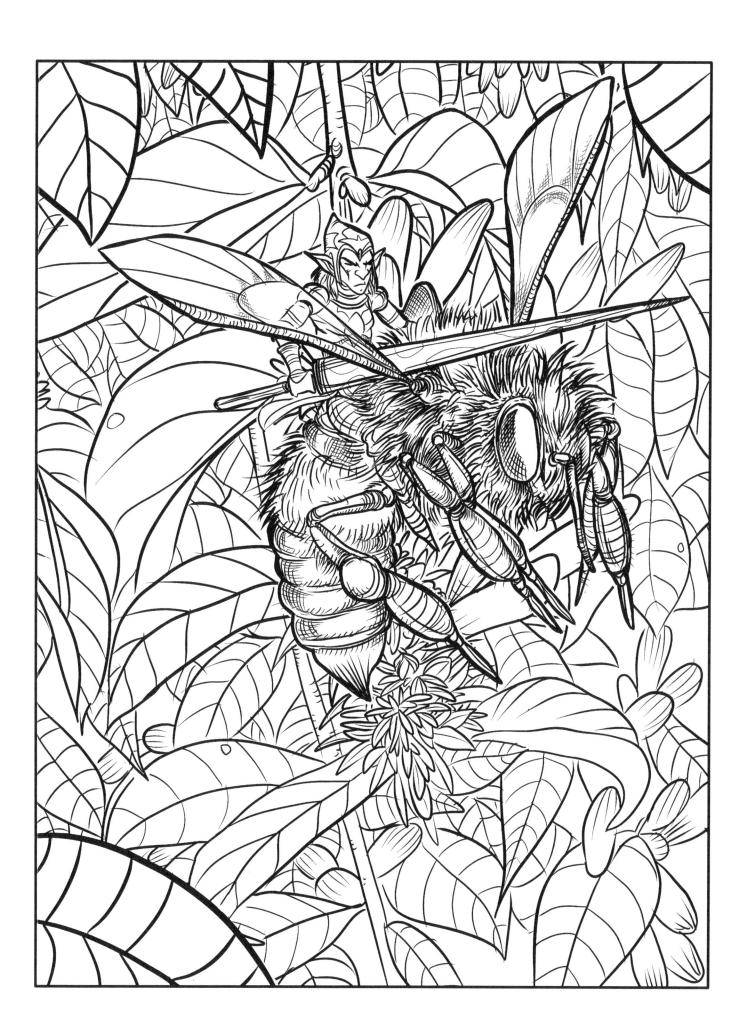

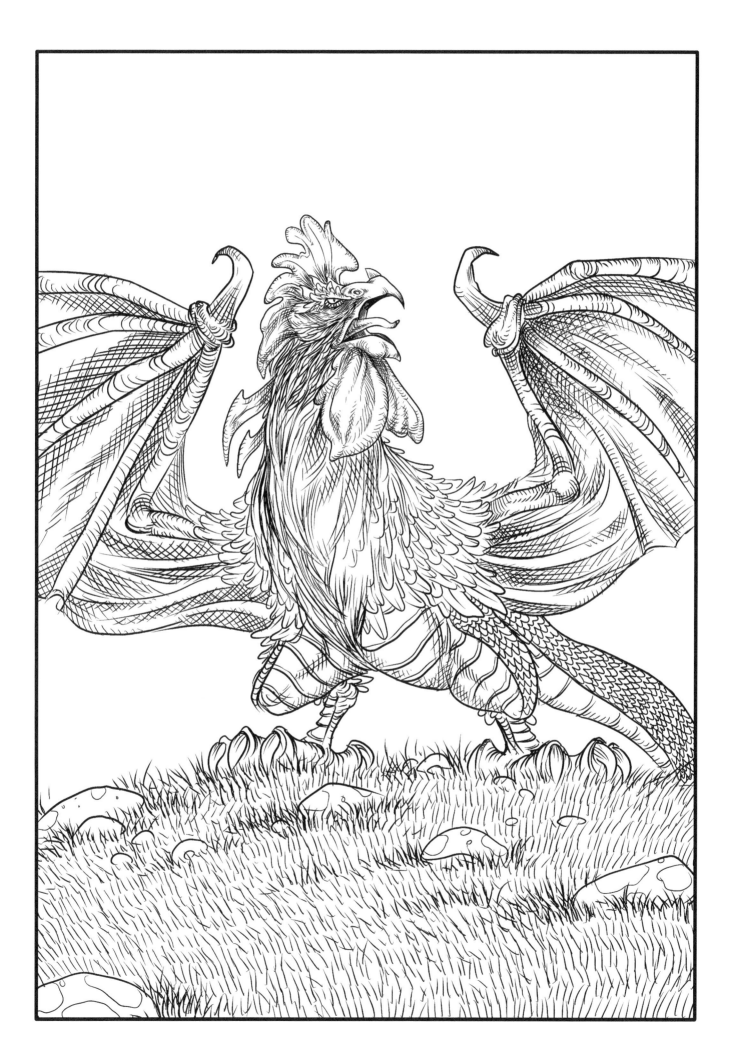

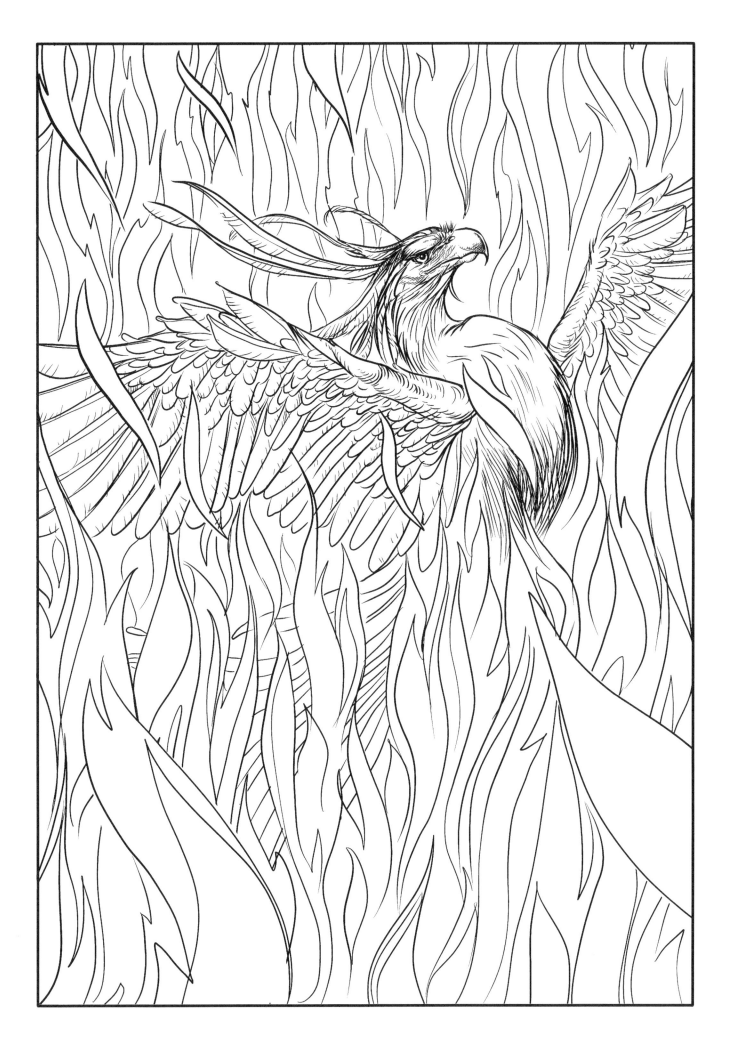

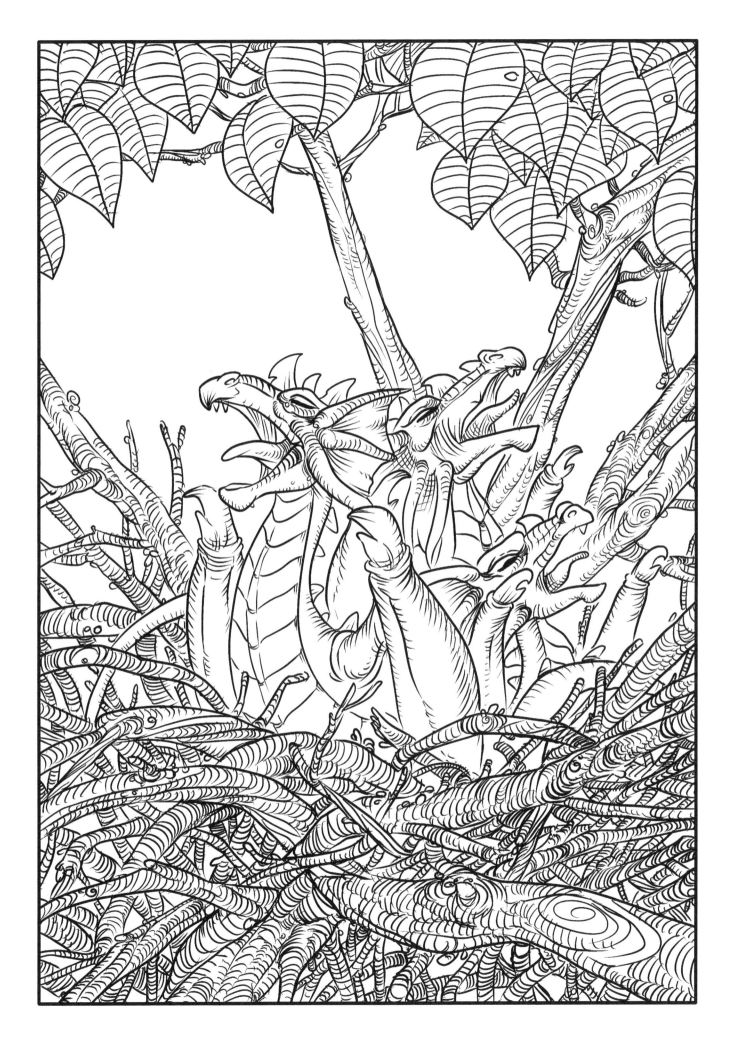

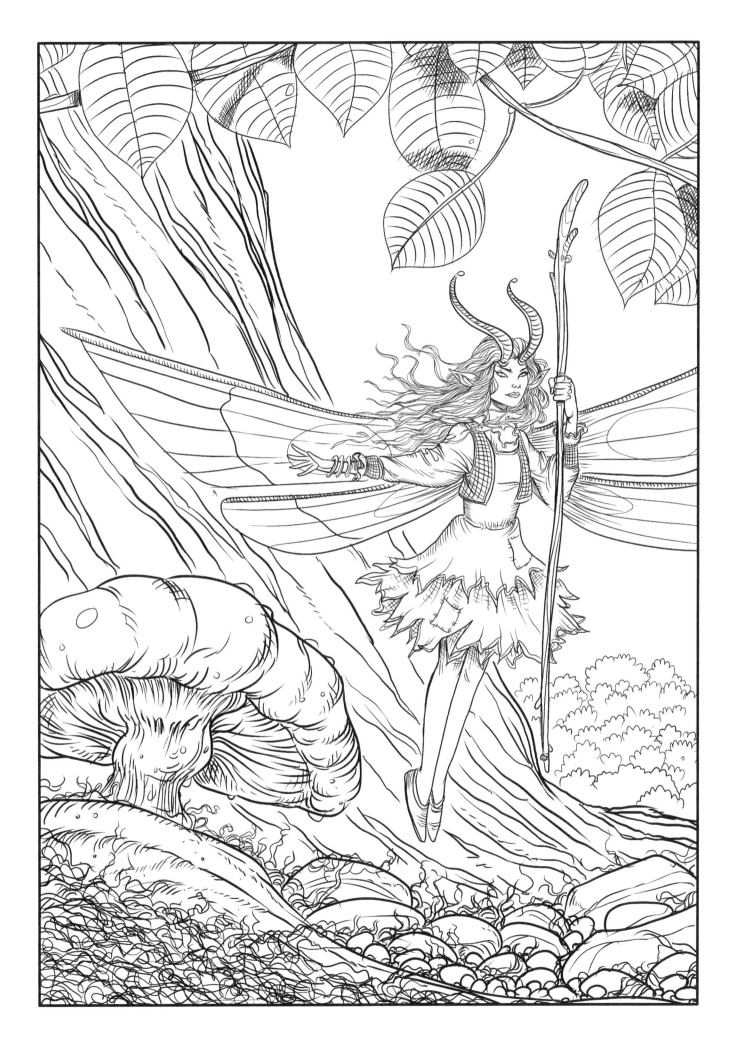

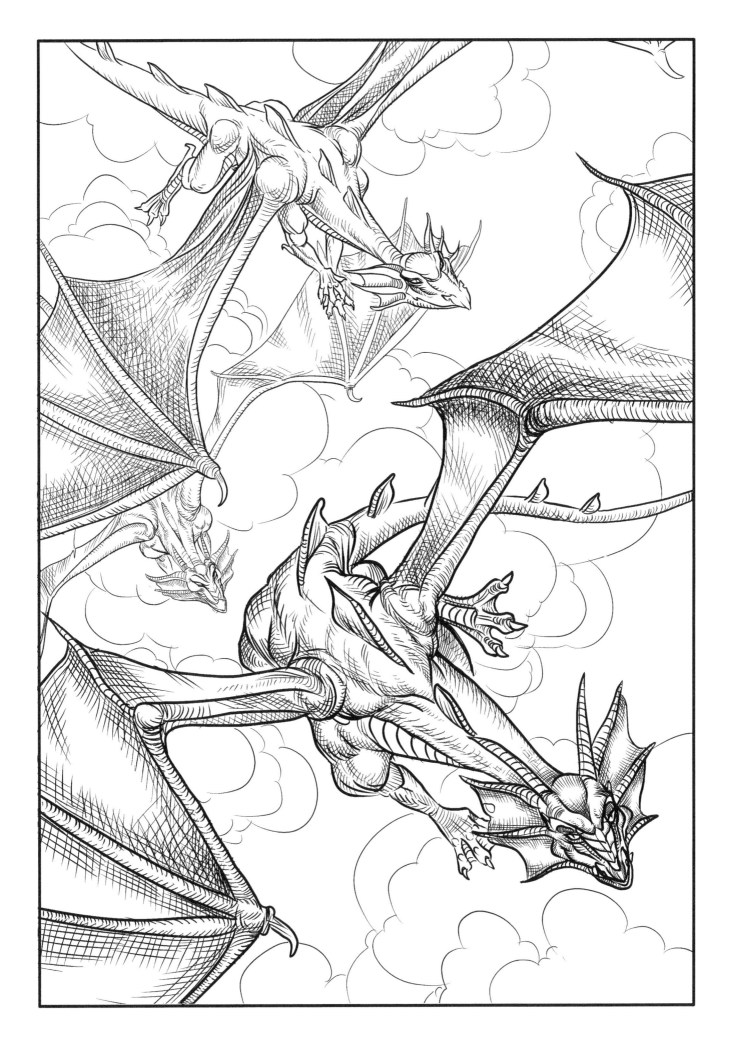

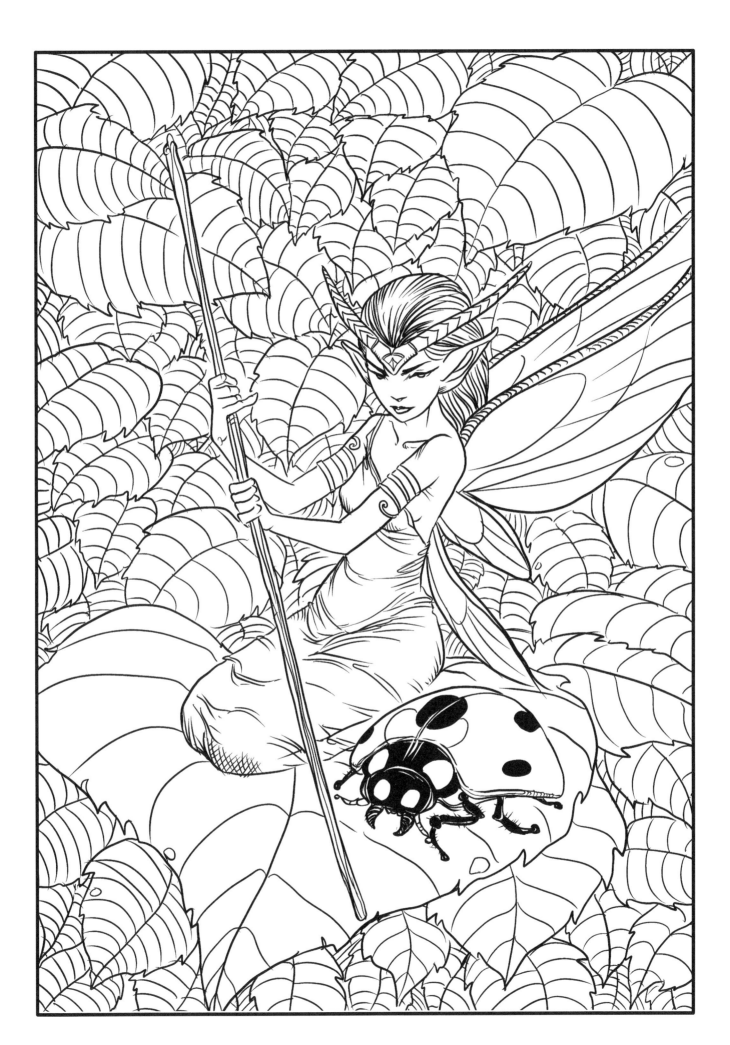

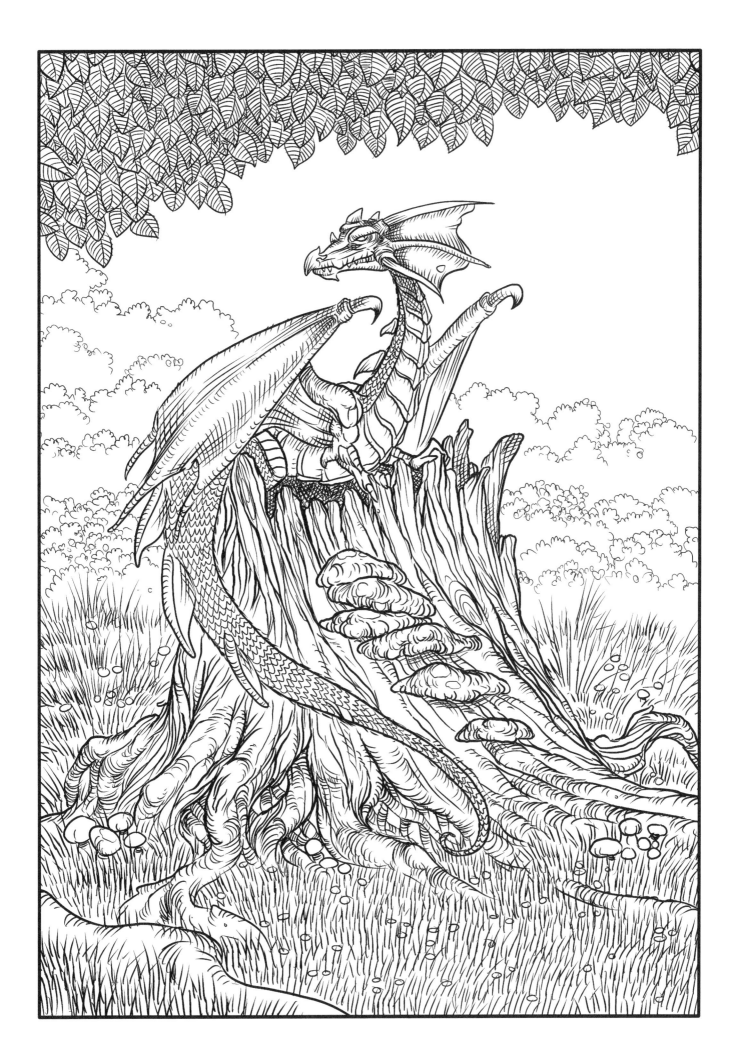

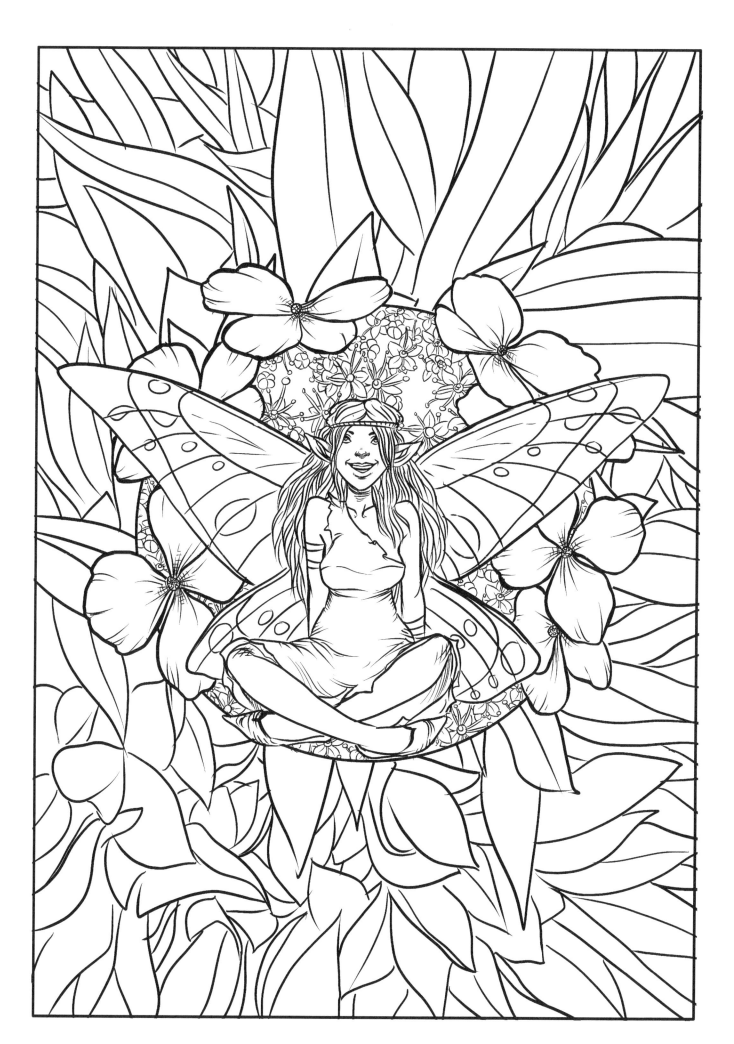

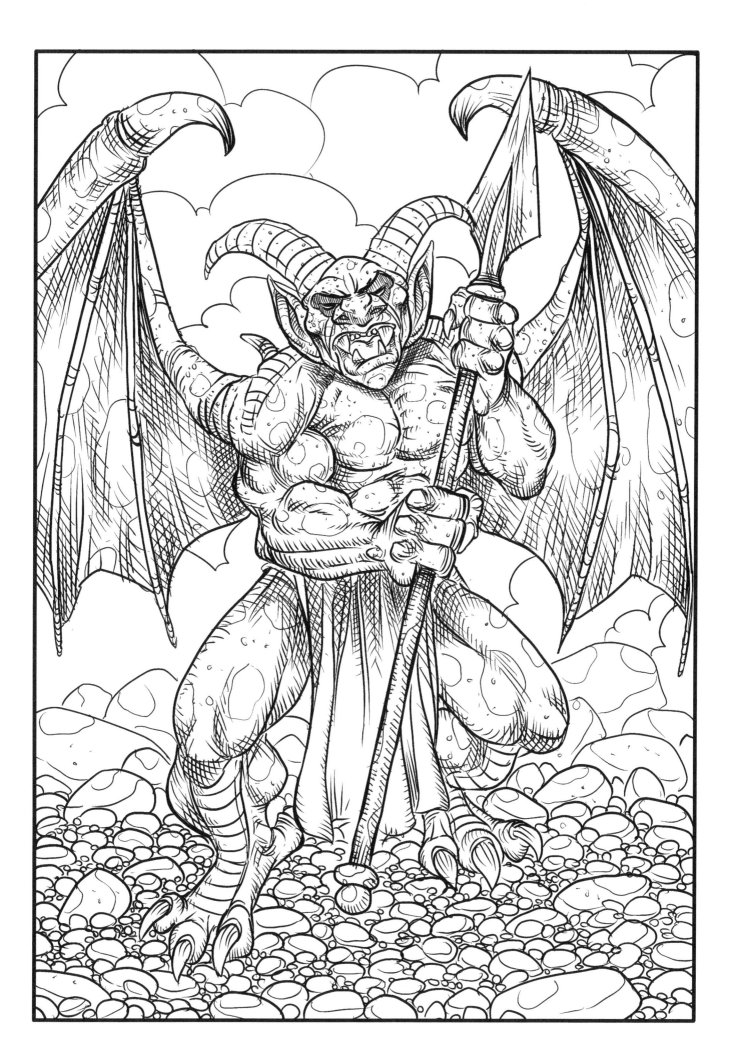

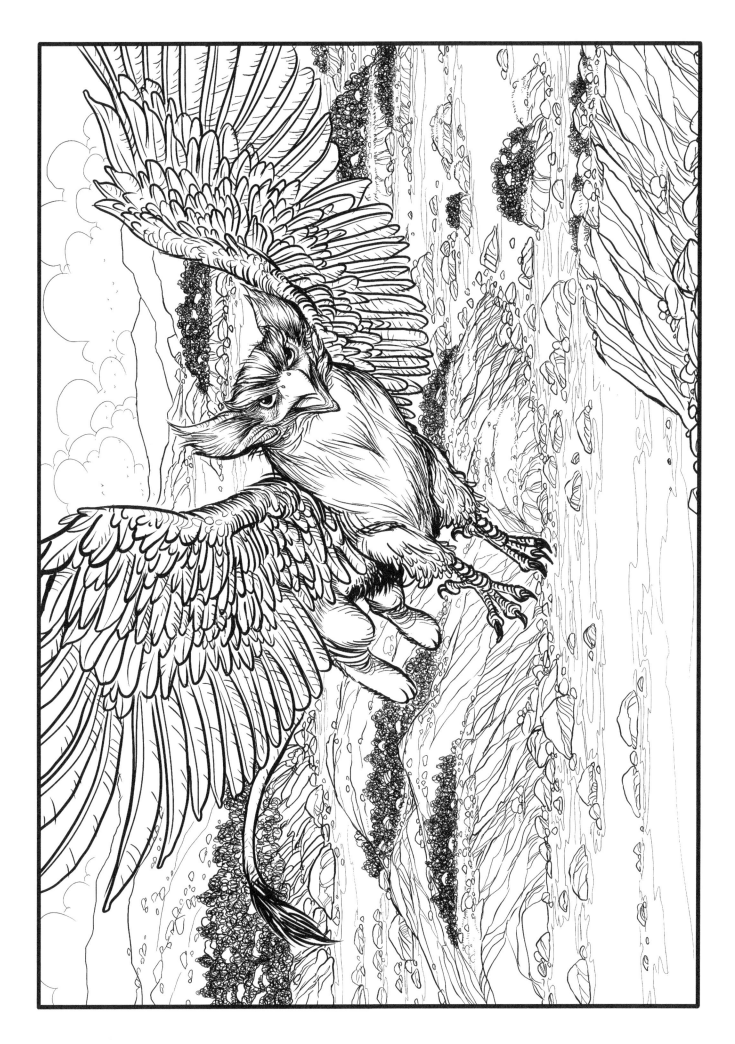

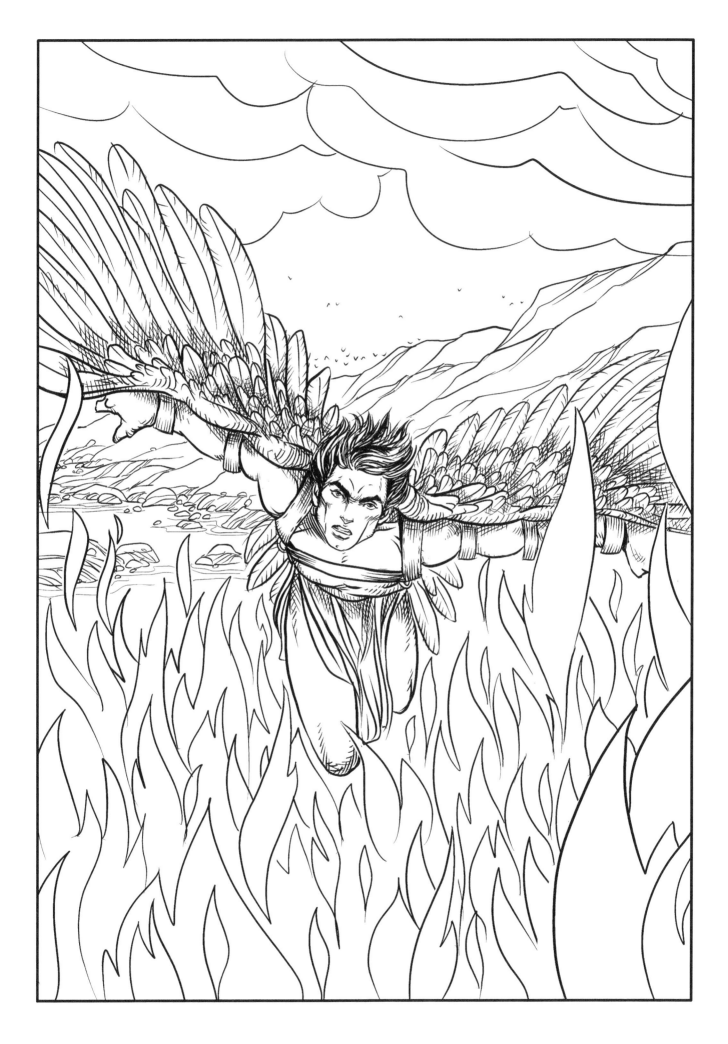

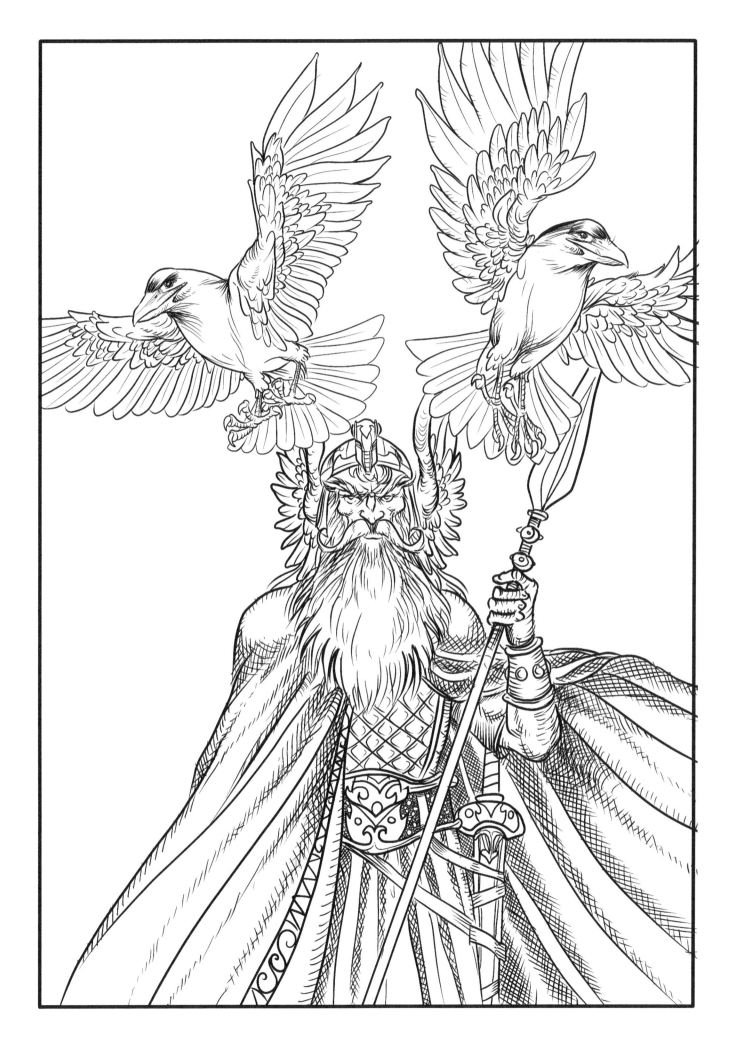

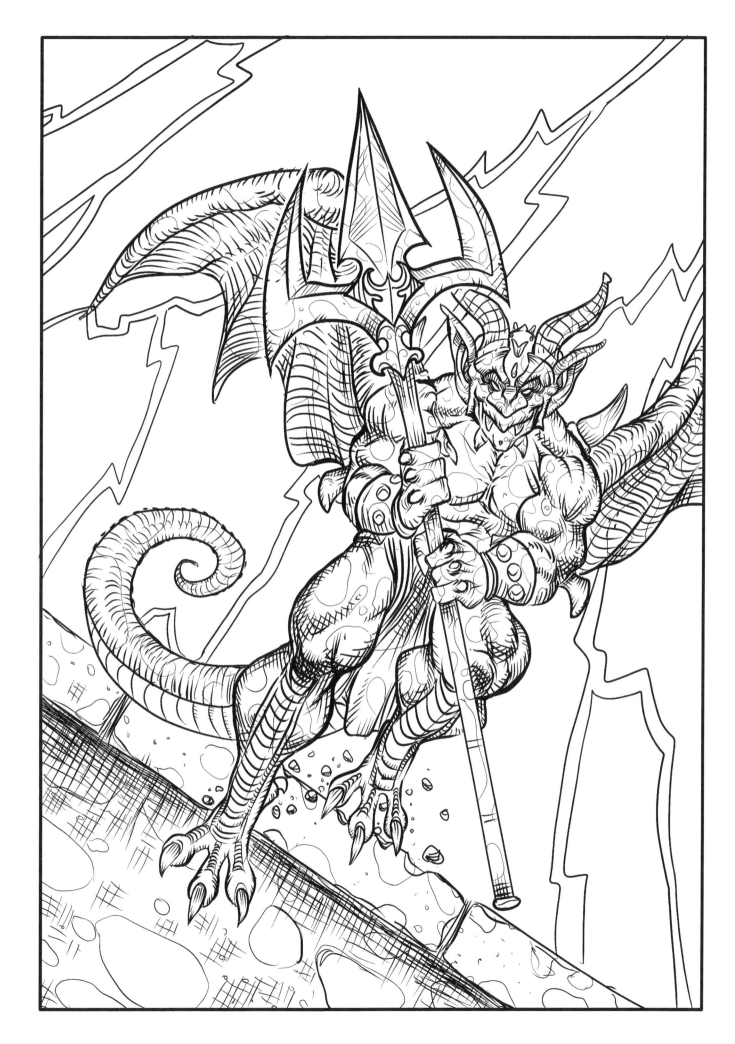

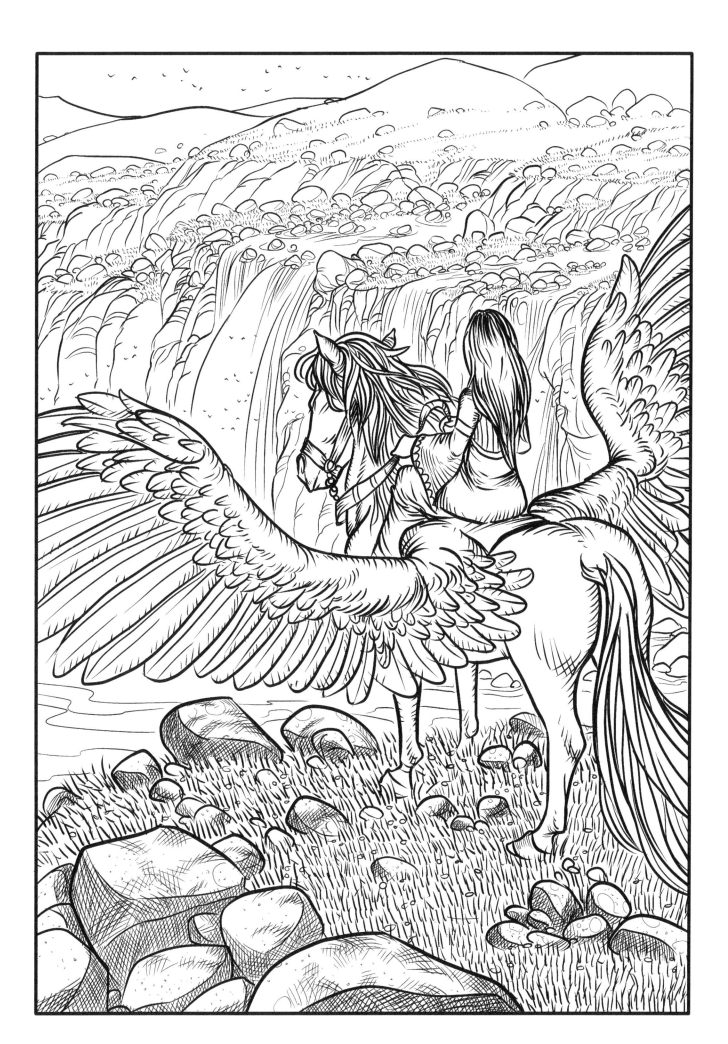

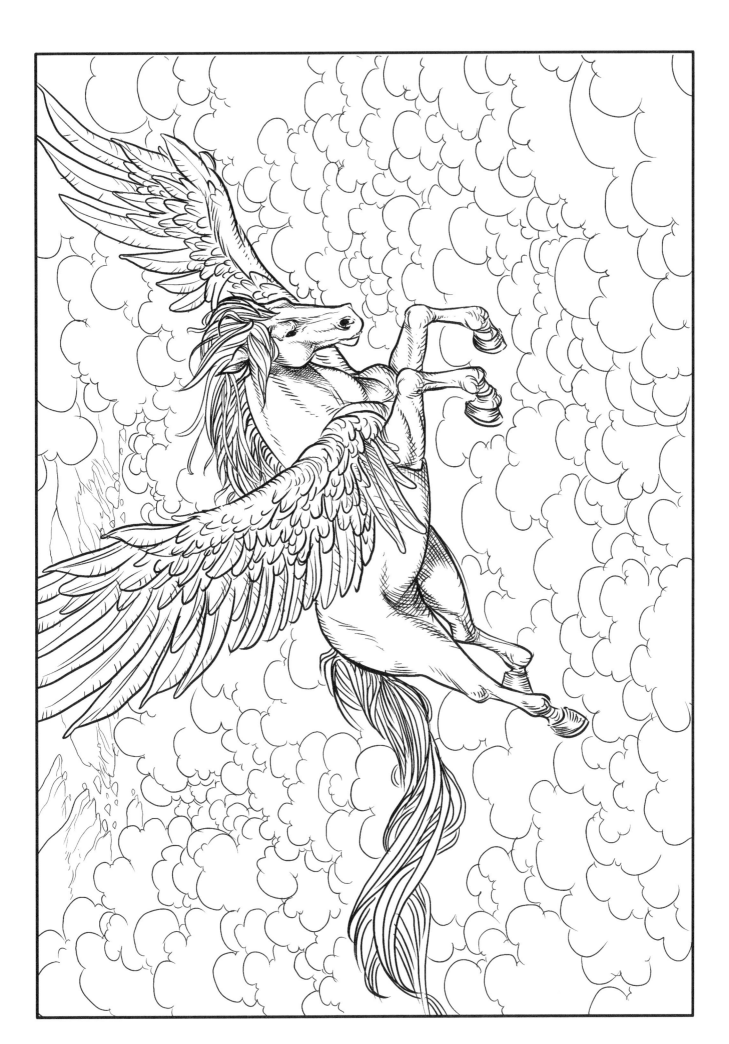

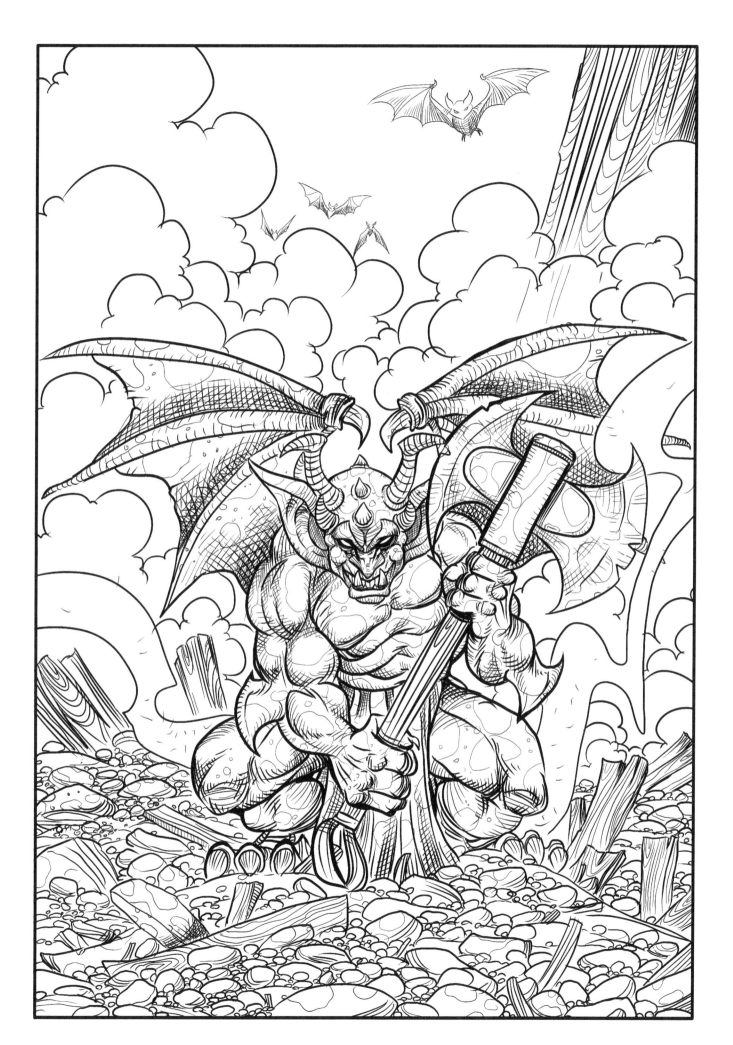

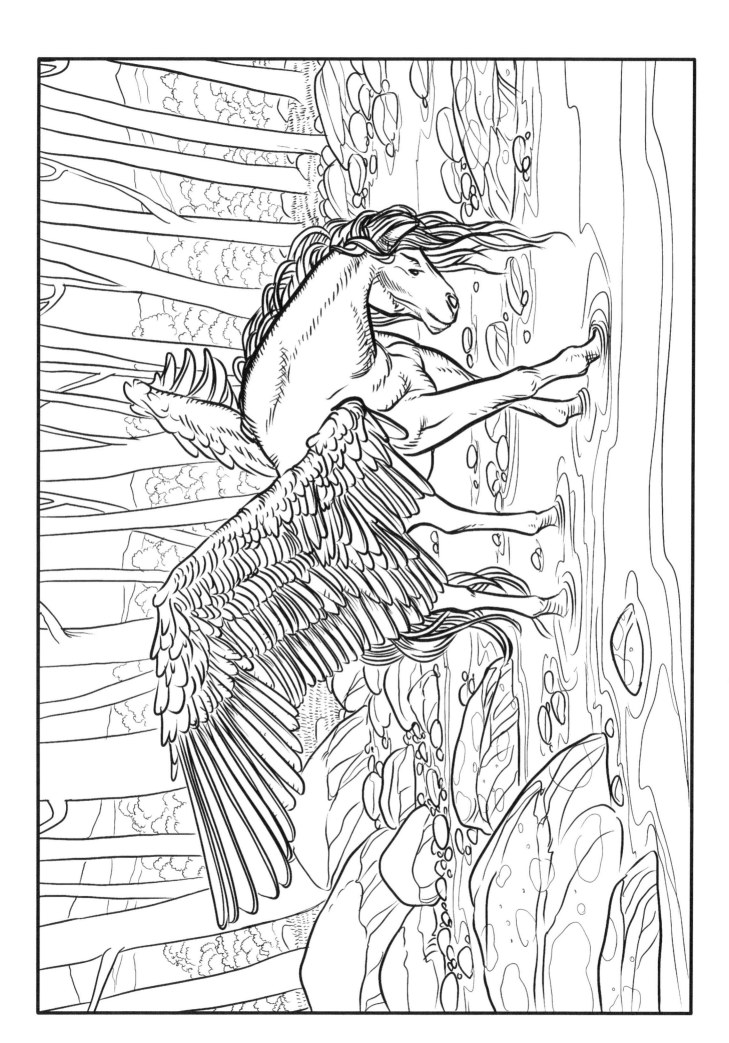

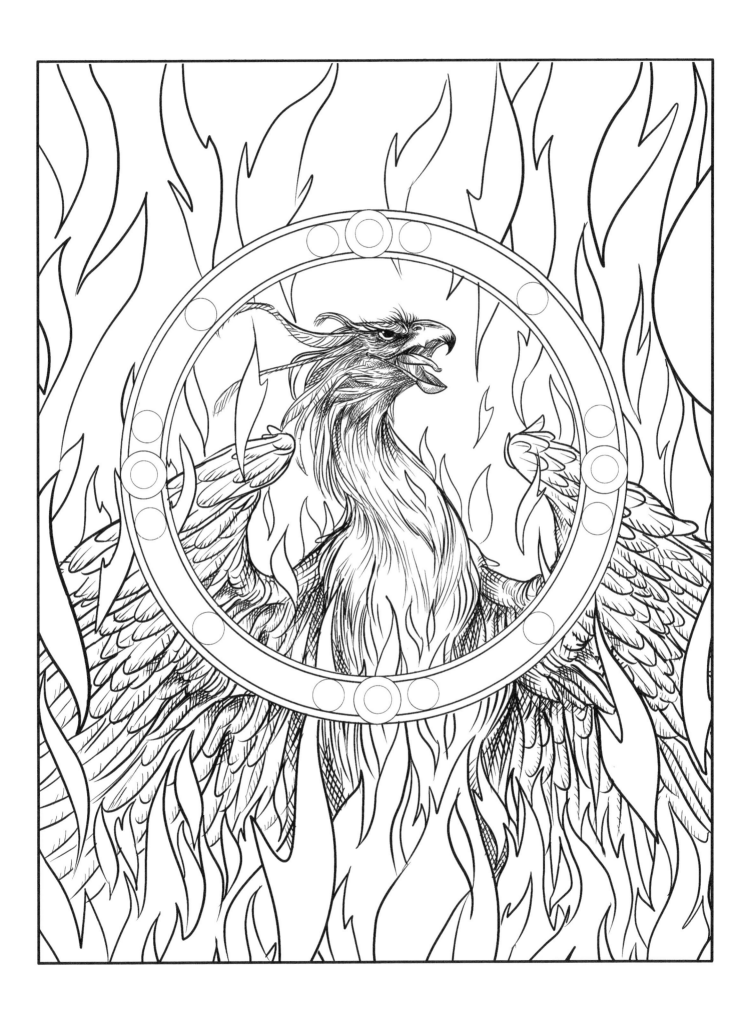

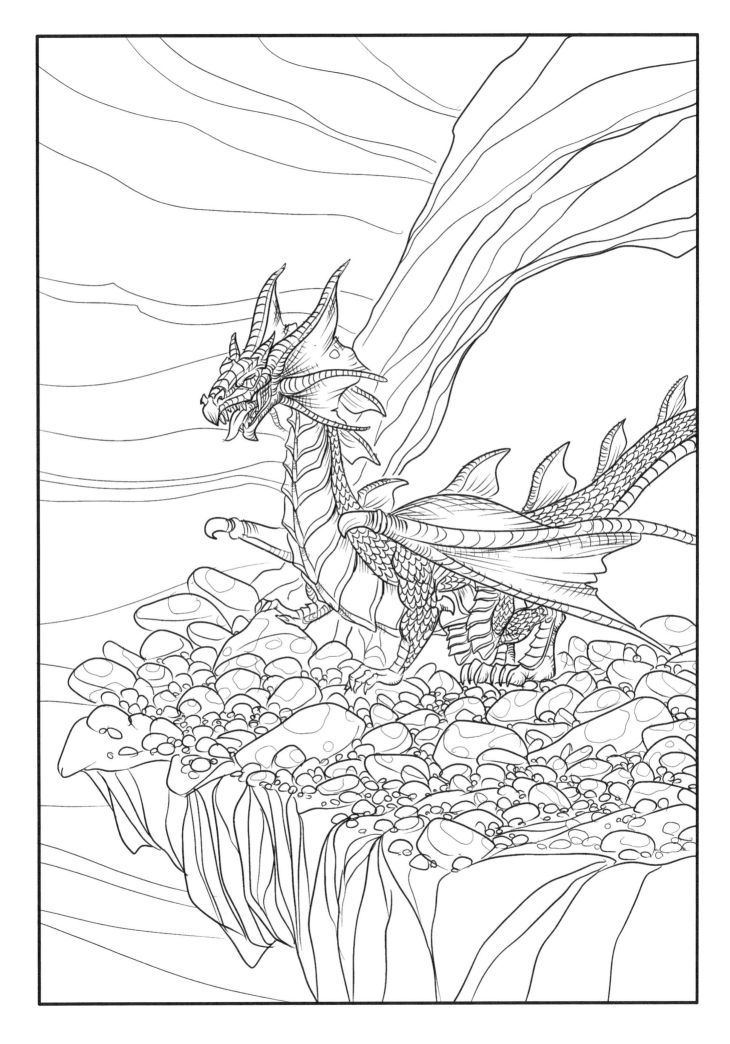

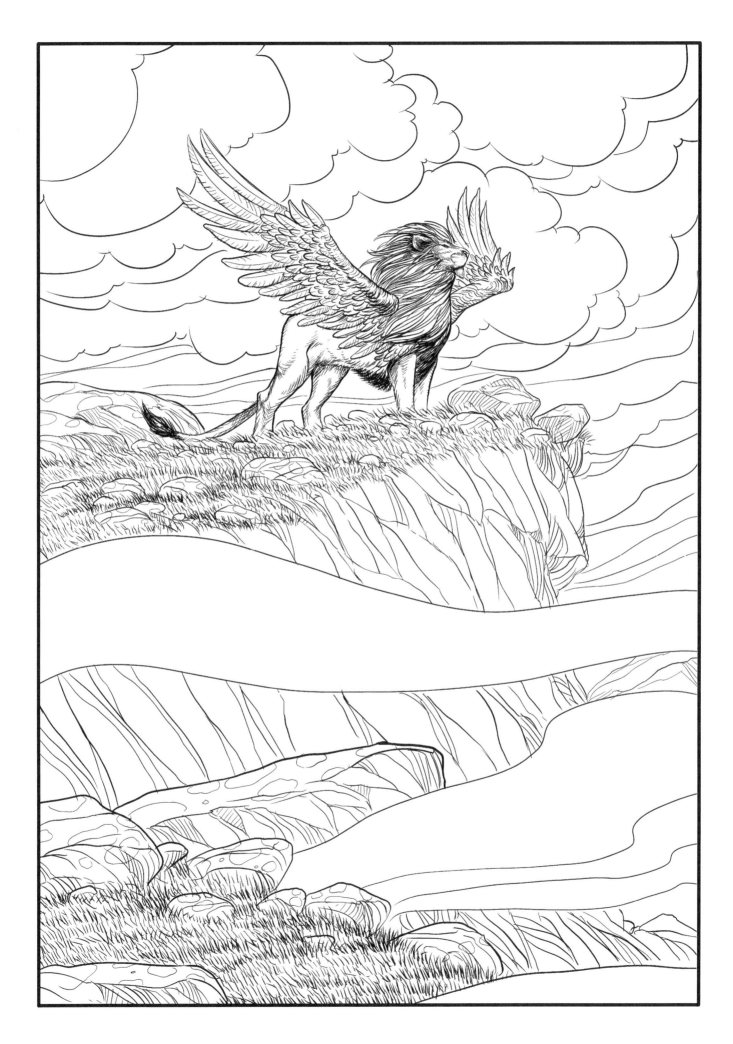

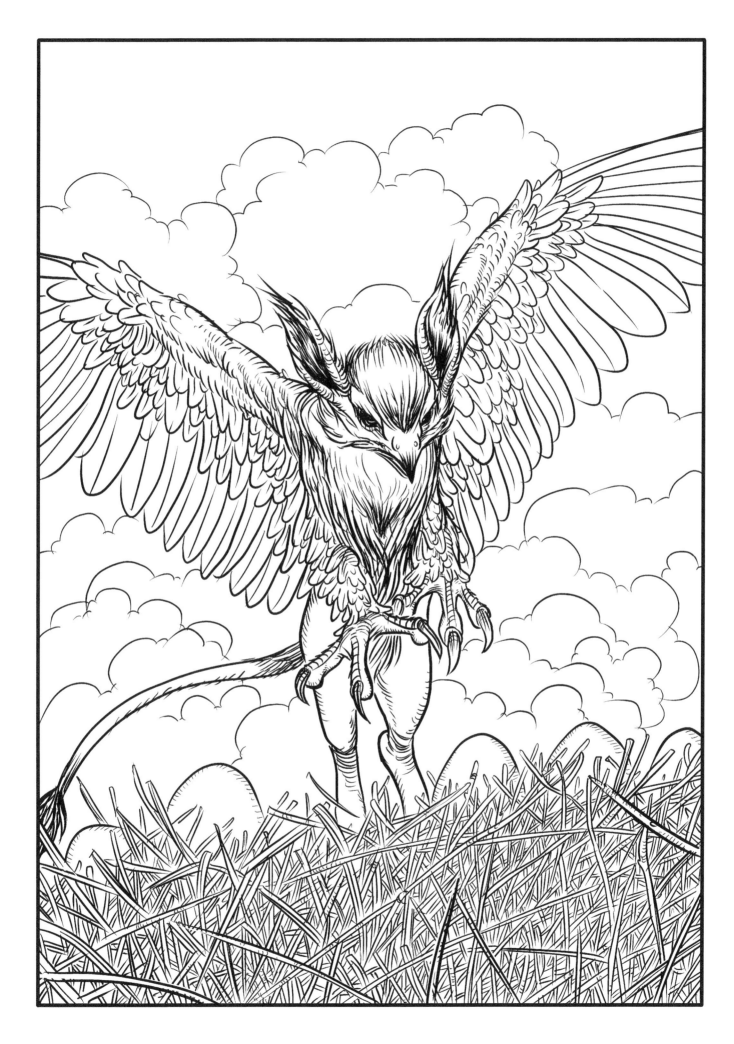

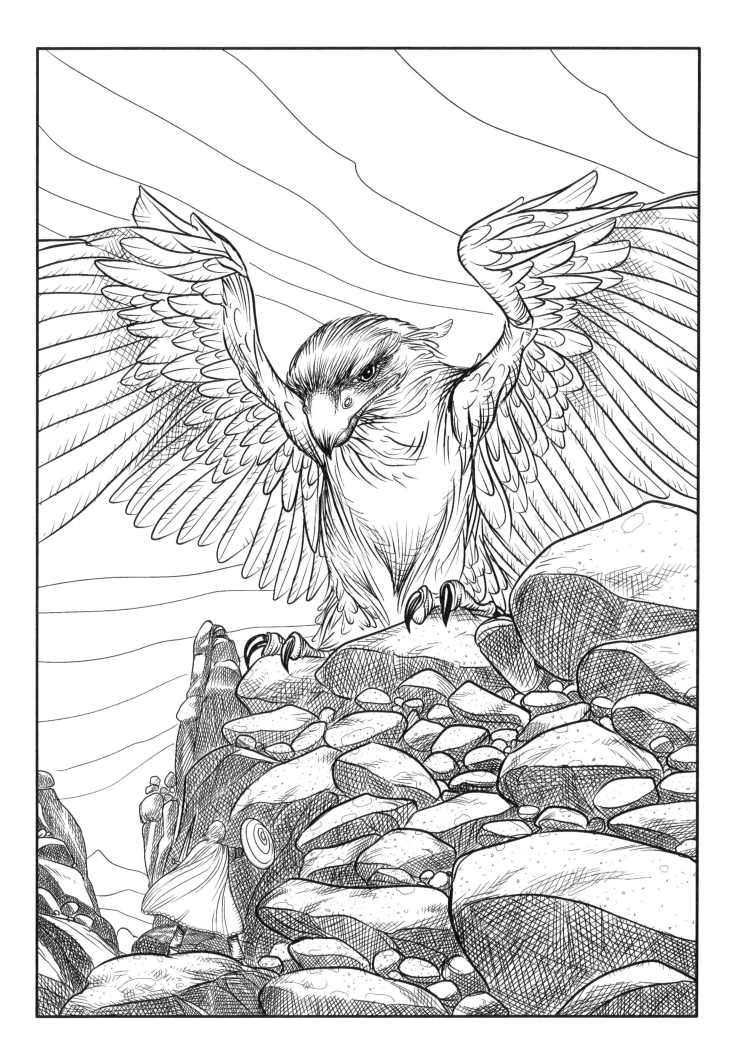

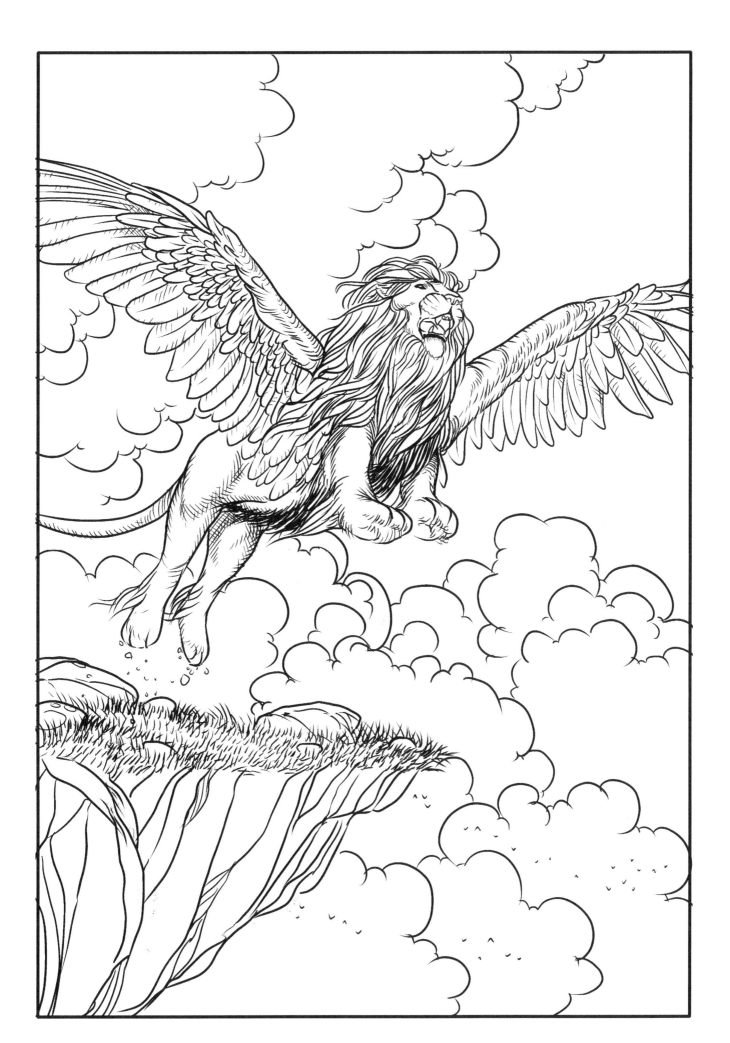